It's the Great Pumpkin,

Charlie Brown

Charles M. Schulz

Random House • New York

Library of Congress Cataloging in Publication Data

Schulz, Charles M. It's the Great Pumpkin, Charlie Brown. SUMMARY: Linus convinces Sally to wait for the Great Pumpkin to arrive on Halloween. [1. Halloween—Fiction] I. Title. PZ7.S38877It [Fic] 80-10287 ISBN: 0-394-84460-2 (trade);
0-394-94460-7 (lib. bdg.)

Manufactured in the United States of America   1 2 3 4 5 6 7 8 9 0

That's just the pumpkin we need, Linus.

Aaaaguh! You didn't tell me you were going to kill it!

Who are you writing to, Linus?

The Great Pumpkin.
On Halloween night
the Great Pumpkin
rises out of the
pumpkin patch.
Then he flies
through the air
with his bag of
toys for all
the children.

You must be crazy. When are you going to stop believing in something that isn't true?

When *you* stop believing in that fellow with the red suit and the white beard who goes, "Ho! Ho! Ho!"

We're obviously separated by denominational differences.

Not again! Writing a letter to a stupid pumpkin? You make me the laughingstock of the neighborhood. All they talk about is my little brother who always writes to the Great Pumpkin. You'd better cut it out right now or I'll pound you!

There are three things I've learned never to discuss with people—religion, politics, and the Great Pumpkin.

You're wasting your time. The Great Pumpkin is a fake.

What are you doing, Linus?

I'd rather not say.
You might laugh.

Oh, I'd never laugh
at you, Linus. You're
so intelligent.

I'm writing to the Great Pumpkin. On Halloween night, the Great Pumpkin rises out of the pumpkin patch and flies through the air. He brings toys to all the good little children everywhere. Wouldn't you like to sit with me in the pumpkin patch on Halloween night and wait for the Great Pumpkin?

Oh I'd love to, Linus.

What's going on here? What are you trying to do to my little sister?

Hey, I got an invitation to Violet's Halloween party.

It's the first time I've ever been invited to a party.

Charlie Brown, if you got an invitation it was a mistake. There were two lists: one of people to invite, and the other of people not to invite. You must have been put on the wrong list.

A person should always choose a costume that is in direct contrast to her own personality.

Is Linus taking you to the party, Lucy?

That stupid blockhead of a brother of mine is out in the pumpkin patch, making a fool of himself.

He's going to miss the trick or treating *and* the party.

I'd like to go trick or treating with you, but I don't know how to do it.

All you have to do is walk up to a house, ring the doorbell, and say, "Trick or treat!"

Are you sure it's legal? I wouldn't want to be accused of taking part in a rumble.

Where is Charlie Brown?

Here I am. I had a little trouble with the scissors.

They'll never think it's me under here.

Hello, Pigpen. Glad you could make it.

How did you know it was me?

Hi, Linus. We're going trick or treating, and then over to Violet's for a big Halloween party.

You blockhead! You're going to miss all the fun just like last year.

Don't talk like that. The Great Pumpkin will come here because I have the most sincere pumpkin patch and he respects sincerity.

Do you really think he'll come?

Tonight the Great Pumpkin rises out of the pumpkin
patch and he flies through the air to bring toys to all the
children of the world.

That's a good story.

All right! Once and for all, we're going. We can't wait for you all night.

I'm glad to see you back, Sally. We'll just sit here in this pumpkin patch and you'll see the Great Pumpkin with your own eyes. Each year the Great Pumpkin rises out of the pumpkin patch he thinks is the most sincere. He's got to pick this one. He's *got* to. I don't see how a pumpkin patch could be more sincere than this one. Looking all around, there is not a sign of hypocrisy. Nothing but sincerity as far as the eye can see.

Trick or treat!

Can I have an extra piece of candy for my stupid little brother? He couldn't come with us because he's sitting in a pumpkin patch, waiting for the Great Pumpkin.

It's so embarrassing to have to ask for something extra for that blockhead Linus.

I got five pieces of candy!

Boy, I got six cookies!

I got a rock.

Here are those two blockheads,
still sitting in a pumpkin patch!

You've missed trick or treating,
and now you're going to miss the
Halloween party.

What a way to spend Halloween!

You think you're so smart! Just wait until the
Great Pumpkin comes. He'll be here. You can
bet on that! Linus knows what he's talking about.
Linus knows what he's doing.

All right, where is he?

He'll be here.

I hope so! I have a reputation to think of, you know. And just think of all the fun we're missing.

Just look. Everywhere sincerity as far as the eye can see.

Charlie Brown, would you like to model for us?

Me? You want *me* to model?

Sure, Charlie Brown. You'll be the perfect model.

Turn him around.

If we shape the eyes like this,
and the nose like this, and the
mouth like this . . .

Thank you, Charlie Brown. You were a perfect model.

All right, let's bob for apples.
I'll show you how to do it.

Yeah, Lucy, you should be good at this. You have the perfect mouth for it.

Bleh! My lips touched dog lips!

Bluuch! Uuch! Poison dog lips!

If anyone had told me I'd be waiting in a pumpkin patch on Halloween night, I'd have said they were crazy.

Just think, Sally. When the Great Pumpkin rises out of the pumpkin patch, we'll be here to see him.

What's that? What's that?

I hear the Great Pumpkin!

There he is! There he is!

It's the Great Pumpkin! He's rising out of the pumpkin patch!

What happened? Did I see him?
What did he leave us? Did he
leave us any toys?

What a fool I was!

I spent the whole night waiting for the Great Pumpkin when I could have been out trick or treating. Halloween's over and I missed it!

You blockhead! You kept me up all night waiting for the Great Pumpkin. And all that came was a beagle! I could have had candy apples and gum and cookies and money and all sorts of things. But no. I had to listen to you! Trick or treating comes only once a year. And I missed it by sitting in a pumpkin patch with a blockhead!

I'm going to sue you!

You've heard about the fury of a
woman scorned, haven't you?

Well, that's nothing compared to the fury of a woman
who has been cheated out of trick or treating.

Hey, aren't you going to wait to greet the Great Pumpkin?
Huh? It won't be long now. If the Great Pumpkin comes,
I'll still put in a good word for you.

Good grief! I said "*if.*" I meant *when* he comes! I'm doomed. One little
slip like that could cause the Great Pumpkin to pass you by.

Oh Great Pumpkin, where are you?

Well, another Halloween
has come and gone. . . .
I don't understand it.
I went trick or treating
and all I got was a bag
full of rocks.

I suppose you spent all
night in the pumpkin patch,
and the Great Pumpkin never
showed up. Well, don't take
it too hard, Linus. I've
done a lot of stupid things
in my life too.

Stupid? What do you
mean stupid?

Just wait till next year, Charlie Brown. You'll see. Next year
at this time, I'll find the patch that is real sincere and I'll sit
in that pumpkin patch until the Great Pumpkin appears. He'll rise
out of that pumpkin patch and he'll fly through the air with a bag
of toys.

The Great Pumpkin
will appear and I'll
be waiting for him! I'll
be there. I'll be sitting
there in the pumpkin
patch. Just you wait,
Charlie Brown.